Sad Snake

Written by Anna Cowper
Illustrated by Amy Lane

Collins

Who and what is in this story?

Listen and say 🎧①

Tom

Lola

snake

Download the audio at www.collins.co.uk/839697

zebras

lion

It's Lola's birthday. Lola's dad gives her a toy snake.

She loves it!

At night, Lola sleeps with her snake.
She has a dream.

The snake is sad. There are no other snakes here.

Tom says, "Let's take it home to its friends!"

Tom and Lola go to look for the snake's friends.

Lola says, "Let's go, snake! Let's find your friends!"

7

Zebras live here.
Do snakes live here, too?
Tom says, "Oh no! There's a lion."

Tom helps Lola and her snake climb the tree.

There are lots of birds in this tree.
And monkeys, too!

There's a BIG spider.
Lola's snake doesn't like spiders!

Pandas live here. Tom loves
baby pandas.

Do snakes live here, too?

This is the panda's dad.
He's not happy!

Lola says, "Let's go!"

Look at the water!
Tom says, "Let's swim!"
Can snakes swim?

Oh no!
There are lots of hippos.
Lola says, "Let's go!"

Do snakes like caves?
Whose eyes are these?

Lola says, "Oh no! It's a bear!"
Tom says, "Run!"

Look! There are lots of snakes here.
They like the sun.

Lola says, "Say hello to your friends, snake."

Lola's snake is happy here.
This is its home.

Lola says, "Goodbye snake!"

Good morning, Lola!
Good morning, snake!

Picture dictionary

Listen and repeat

bear

bird

hippo

lion

monkey

panda

snake

spider

zebra

1 Look and order the story

2 Listen and say

Download a reading guide for parents and teachers at
www.collins.co.uk/839697

Collins

Published by Collins
An imprint of HarperCollins*Publishers*
Westerhill Road
Bishopbriggs
Glasgow
G64 2QT

HarperCollins*Publishers*
1st Floor, Watermarque Building
Ringsend Road
Dublin 4
Ireland

William Collins' dream of knowledge for all began with the publication of his first book in 1819.

A self-educated mill worker, he not only enriched millions of lives, but also founded a flourishing publishing house. Today, staying true to this spirit, Collins books are packed with inspiration, innovation and practical expertise. They place you at the centre of a world of possibility and give you exactly what you need to explore it.

© HarperCollins*Publishers* Limited 2020

10 9 8 7 6 5 4 3 2

ISBN 978-0-00-839697-8

Collins® and COBUILD® are registered trademarks of HarperCollins*Publishers* Limited

www.collins.co.uk/elt

All rights reserved. No part of this publication may be reproduced, stored in a retrieval system, or transmitted in any form by any means, electronic, mechanical, photocopying, recording or otherwise, without the prior written permission of the Publisher or a licence permitting restricted copying in the United Kingdom issued by the Copyright Licensing Agency Ltd, 5th Floor, Shackleton House, 4 Battle Bridge Lane, London SE1 2HX.

British Library Cataloguing in Publication Data

A catalogue record for this publication is available from the British Library.

All rights reserved. No part of this book may be reproduced, stored in a retrieval system, or transmitted in any form or by any means, electronic, mechanical, photocopying, recording or otherwise, without the prior permission in writing of the Publisher. This book is sold subject to the conditions that it shall not, by way of trade or otherwise, be lent, re-sold, hired out or otherwise circulated without the Publisher's prior consent in any form of binding or cover other than that in which it is published and without a similar condition including this condition being imposed on the subsequent purchaser.

Author: Anna Cowper
Illustrator: Amy Lane (Beehive)
Series editor: Rebecca Adlard
Publishing manager: Lisa Todd
Product managers: Jennifer Hall and Caroline Green
In-house editor: Alma Puts Keren
Project manager: Emily Hooton
Editor: Tessie Papadopoulou-Dalton
Proofreaders: Natalie Murray and Michael Lamb
Cover designer: Kevin Robbins
Typesetter: 2Hoots Publishing Services Ltd
Audio produced by id audio, London
Reading guide author: Emma Wilkinson
Production controller: Rachel Weaver
Printed and bound by: GPS Group, Slovenia

MIX
Paper from
responsible sources
FSC™ C007454

FSC
www.fsc.org

This book is produced from independently certified FSC™ paper to ensure responsible forest management.

For more information visit: **www.harpercollins.co.uk/green**

Download the audio for this book and a reading guide for parents and teachers at www.collins.co.uk/839697